Into the Darkness

Into the Darkness

A Legend

The Scales *Adam Zilm*

Rev. date: 09/08/2021

To order additional copies of this book, contact:
Xlibris
844-714-8691
www.Xlibris.com
Orders@Xlibris.com
834426

Contents

Chapter One

New Hope

Superior presences of both the holy flames and the bitter, cold darkness surround her little soul. The only sound to be heard is that of her little heart as it pounds from the terrors that haunt her!

A wrathful voice:

> "The world shall be plundered in darkness,
> Where evil shall stealth with their prowess.
> The darkness has become thick.
> Evil is the oldest kind of sick.
> It's also the best holy fire wick!"

> Her heart pounded more furiously.
> She needed help indefinitely!

A dark, twisted voice:

> "Thou shall be in my grasp,
> Yet thy soul and all its seams are what thee have bet.
> I'll forever be in thy dreams, so thou will never forget . . . thy screams!
> Then we will bleed thee to watch thee squirm,
> Watching thee wiggle like a little worm!"

Her little heart in trouble, and the mother in a state of emergency.
Her daughter's night terrors a matter of urgency!
The doctors draw sweat as they fought for her life,
As they cut her mother with the knife.
Soon, though, it was time to rejoice,
For this girl, Seaira, will soon have a voice.
Then came the doctor bearing good news,
Life in the girl with only minor issues.
Blindness and skin sensitivity,
A new life strengthens this family's elasticity.

Years pass. The family of three enjoys Christmases and Easters, and they give thanks. All is normal, or as normal as it may seem; maybe normal is but a dream.

Soon she was going to school with her older brother Kaydon, but he is tasked much with her protection. Her blindness is not only her curse; it is also his. Bullies find her an easy target, and he becomes her guardian, her protector, and her way to guidance. But this burden starts making him bitter, and soon anger filled within him. Then the day came when he abandons her!

Seaira: I like it when you read this to me, but you don't have to make reference to me while reading it. Just say it to me as it is written, as if you were reading to someone else! I think we will get answers faster, and no one has read me a story in a long time, so I do really enjoy this!

Fate: As thou wish

Kaydon wanted to pretend she no longer exists.
As he ventured over the mountains into its mists,
Seaira was lost and thrown around after school,
Kids just acting like a fool.
This sixth sense may be a blessing,
But Seaira's problems just started manifesting.
She felt their intention
Already going in the wrong direction.

A blind girl should not have the ability to dodge attacks!
This spooks the others, exposing their cracks,
Thus causing her more pain,
Maybe not all in vain!

Kaydon returns after his sister has run off and starts asking, "What happened?"

The bullies respond, "The blind creep can dodge."

Filled with rage,
Battle he did engage.
He is never going to get victory,
But he still has to look for her in the vicinity!
Returning home with all their bruises,
They spat out a whole pile of excuses.

The mother feeds them and comforts them, but their troubles are just getting started. The next morning, feeling awkwardly safe sitting at the table, she hears the usual clicking, clattering, and scuffing around. It is a basic morning rise for a family of humans, but it is the news that carries unsettling words of war.

Leaders are slithering.
Control they are craving.
In power they are bathing!
Anxiety builds from the anticipation
Of terrorizing devastation.
A struggle of domination,
Reality settling in further,
As the news of war echoes through the channel converter.

Desperate reporter:
"I do not have much time. We were not allowed to say anything! So I did some digging, and there is much . . ."

The family accepted the chip
Under the government's whip.
But Seaira took a fit,
Barely avoiding the firing pit.
Then what's a mother supposed to do?
All these hidden secrets leave her with no clue.
When the bombs finally struck,
She barely manages to get food into the family truck.
As they try to speed from the storm,
An enemy showed in an expected form.
Bandits using flying metal, they did shred.
Only thing left is the family and their only loaf of bread.
For then they did crash.
Their metal wagon did smash.
Waking to her motherly cry,
Thinking her babies did die.
Rushing them from the bloody scene,
With no clue of what happened to the men who were so mean.
Lucky they are to find
A group that is truly kind.

A group of good people has banned together to protect one another from the evil that surrounds them. They protect one another with metal projectile weaponry and shelter. Those who can't fight are gatherers, cooks, doctors, and builders—all who help with the stability of the group.

People snapping into their realities,
Just out of puffed-up societies.
So out of touch with their priorities,
Many fall, too weak to stand.
To others, luck was their brand,
But all will eventually burn with their land!

A few days pass; they know a short time of peace. Surrounded by chaos, it doesn't take long before the madness finds them. It's not a matter of if they will die; it's a matter of how that worries them. Will they die in a hail of metal, or will they be captured? Will their death be swift, or will lesser pain become a gift? On one fateful day, the group meets their fate's end.

Seaira, asleep in a dream,
Walking on a beam.
She hears her brother scream,
Feeling too scared to move
But afraid of no evil she must prove.
Then somehow in a cave,
Still trying to be so brave,
In a corner she knelt,
So scared she felt.
As she recites her prayer,
She knows something is there.
Hearing the scrape of a claw,
Just over the chattering of her jaw,
What happens next, she never saw.

She awoke screaming, then runs toward her mother. Then she quickly turned and gave a hug to her brother. She thought she cannot do without one or the other!

Chapter Two

Humans

Bandits appear;
Goods are why they are here.
Food and water
is what brought this group to their slaughter!
So many people in need,
So many to feed,
Now theft is not only for greed,
For bandits need nutrients for their seed.

The mother grabed her children and flees for the mountains. Running from the hail of gunfire, into the rocky mountain range, the mother sees a cave. This cave may be their only salvation. This may be the only place she can keep her children away from the devastation. As they get closer, the mother realizes that the cave is surrounded by mines! Out of options and in need of safe shelter, she comes up with a plan. She will keep her children behind her at a safe point and move forward through the minefield. With any luck, she can make a safe path!

Comforting her children with a soothing voice,
Also preparing them for the worse circumstance of her choice.
If she shall die, then proceed they must,
In case a mine makes their mother's outer crust bust.
A path she did make,
Her nerve to never break!
Just in reach of safety's glee,

Not realizing she is still in a state of emergency!
The final mine in her path
Shows no mercy, only wrath!
Kaydon, seeing her timely demise,
Tells Seaira, "Get into the cave until sunrise."
His next choice comes with no surprise.
Looking into her motherly gaze,
As her eyes begun to haze,
As she moves toward her final phase.
Her brother's mind unraveled
As his thoughts traveled.
No longer will he see for his sister;
Seaira's curse is what made him bitter.
For now, Kaydon travels alone,
Leaving with his bitter tone,
To reunite with her in the courtyard of the dark throne.
Such a sad and lost little one
Seems to be a forever lost son.

The cave may be dark, ridged, damp, and eerie,
But there is a reason to be cheery!
There are a few who watch and are leery,
Just waiting for the judgment of the jury.
Odorless gas fills the chamber,
Meant to put Seaira in a slumber,
Making her easy to encumber.
Falling is all she can remember!
Another dream of fire and wrath,
All within a dark bath.
Skies go black;
Time never goes back!

Chapter Three

The Meeting

Seaira now weeping,
Even when she is sleeping.
She feels the darkness creeping.
Away from rocks, she seems to be leaping,
Yet only ever briefly seeing
While she is dreaming.
Seaira wakes once again, screaming,
Searching for meaning,
For answers she is feigning.
What's the purpose of her being?
Awakening in a room of steel,
Lights like the sun, nice they feel.
The nice warming of the skin
While she waits for the news of her kin.
Seeing both soft and scale,
Hoping to prevail.
Never did most humans think
That there were others in their rink.
Fighting against the same evil,
Teamed up with another type of people.
Truth still under seal,

Will they rise for their big reveal?
She's in a nice, safe facility,
But not built by humanity.
Soon this was her reality.
A nurse enters the room.
Her intention is obvious like a flower's bloom.
How I wish this was a happy tune.
Questions shall be answered soon.
First are the simplest of questions, like her age,
Just checking overall health while going down a page.
She senses the nurse's soul and sees purity,
Here to find a tranquility
All while showing great humility.
Still, something was amiss.
Every now and again, Seaira would hear a hiss.
Many voices she did hear;
This one though was not clear.
She asks to feel the nurse's face.
Where the trust comes from is hard to trace.
Allowing what was always forbidden,
But what's the point of hiding from a harmless kitten?
As Seaira reaches out her hand,
Her words barely did land.

Seaira: "May I?"

Seaira: *I remember that awkward moment. I don't usually do that!*

This unusual faith allows Seaira to touch the side of the nurse's face. The nurse's scaly skin may be tough, ridged, hard, and even sharp at times! This brave girl was only startled, but not alarmed. What Seaira said next sparked an intriguing conversation.

Seaira, with excitement within her voice: "I knew it was all real. I saw your people before in my nightmares. Your people were trying to help us fight back the demons. Then when I heard your voice, I knew it had to be one of you, even though I never heard many voices in my nightmares. And I didn't exactly know. I just had a lucky guess."

Nurse: "How can you have seen us before? You said you were born blind."

Seaira: "It seems I know a lot of things a girl born blind shouldn't know. Like your people range in all sorts of colors just like my people, but your scaly skin makes these colors more vibrant. People have spoken to me about different things in this world, like the moon, sun, trees, rivers, fish, and bears. Of course, not all these things are in my nightmares. Nonetheless, they are usually shocked by my awareness!"

Nurse: "To you, what is a demon?"

Seaira, feeling uneasy, still answers, "In my nightmares, I can see! Demons are the ones who hide in the dark! The darkness makes them hard to see. Some of their souls are so black that they stand out in the darkest of nights! The others, darkness is their camouflage, so I must follow my gut feeling of fear to avoid them. I run so fast but could not get away. Their leader's whispers chill my spine even now! He calls himself the Master of Madness, and I truly fear his rise from the depths below. My human doctor says my mind makes it all up, and my mom thinks it's where I'm smart. That's why my nightmares are so vividly scary, or at least that's what she used to say to me. I heard Mom once crying, worrying about my future, worrying about me 'getting worse.' The next day, I tried reassuring her by saying, 'Don't worry about me, because when the world ends, the angels will protect me. You should be more worried about everyone else because the world is dying, and it's not only our home. The scaly people shared their home with us, and they are not happy with all the harm to our planet. Because of this, everyone may be in danger.' This made Mom burst into tears again, as if she believed even more of what the doctor was saying. I think my mom spent so much time worrying about me that my brother would almost go unnoticed. I know that hurts him, because sometimes, when he would help me from school, he would get angry with me. Kaydon! You guys have to help him. He's lost. I'm sure of it. You must help him."

The nurse, sensing the air once again with her tongue: "I know you're afraid for your brother. We can send someone to try and find him, but these are trying times. Our people are very busy!"

Seaira: "I keep hearing something."

The nurse's tongue, again sensing the air: "Oh, that's my tongue. It is how we smell. Some humans we have interacted with believed we were reading their minds, but really, we were only smelling the natural chemicals that humans release under the effects of different emotions. As we have access to the imagination of the human mind, this accessibility to your minds was placed there by your creators. This gives us a needed camouflage when we have to move among your people."

Seaira: "Our creators! So your people met the angels and maybe even Life himself? *Wow!*"

Nurse: "No, child, we are unsure where humans get the idea of angels and demons, but your creators are much like yourselves, just taller, bigger, stronger, faster, and way smarter!"

Seaira: "Hey . . . that's not very nice!"

Nurse: "I am merely speaking the truth. Your creators made you this way for slaves or frontline soldiers. They purposely placed altercations within your DNA, some of which still evident after all these years. Your creator's planet was dying, so they built a big ship called New Opportunity's Archive Home Searcher, which then sailed toward Earth, the closest neighboring planet that can maintain life. They thought this planet was only occupied by big beasts humans know as the dinosaurs, but we already ruled these lands. We evolved into intelligent beings from our closest cousin, the raptor, which was many years ago! When they arrived, it started a massive war, but our technology was great, and we had many hidden underground bases. Trying to control our planet became an impossible task. Through this war though, many of your ancestors managed to escape! That is when your creators had to signal a retreat. On their way back home, they sent a final attack in the form of a meteor, aiming it at a very large sulfur deposit in a place human's call Mexico. This caught our Earth ablaze. This fire made the sky black, blocking out the sun. That is when the Ice Age came, changing the development and face of this planet to the place we all call home, thus making extinct the dinosaurs!"

Seaira: "Wow! So that's what really happened. Well, I guess people were not wrong. It was a meteor, but it just wasn't an accident! But if the world was on fire, how did the cavemen survive?"

Nurse: "Well, it was due to our interference. A council meeting was called to decide the fate of your ancestors, who were still among us after the war. It was decided that this war was no fault to the early humans. That war was not their decision, so they were deemed innocent, and that is when we tried to fix the biological damage placed by your creators! The progress was slow, but once the world was inhabitable again, we released you into the wild, and ever since, we were rooting for your success!"

Seaira: "What do you mean 'were'? Do you guys still hope we succeed?"

Nurse: "I am afraid, child, that once again, a council meeting has been called to decide the fate of humans, but this time, they are not so innocent and will not be judged as such! We have allowed you to evolve naturally, and now we see humans still have hate in them as their creators did! All these years, we watched as humans slaughter one another over simple racial differences and beliefs. We watched the disgraces of humans, and now we see!"

Seaira: "Have you lost all faith? Is there really no hope? There's a lot of good people suffering right now who just need help, people who just need a chance!"

Nurse: "I am afraid even if I believed it to be true, it's not up to me, and the fact that they're still breathing proves that they had a chance to change. Not giving humans a chance would be killing all of your ancestors thousands of years ago."

Seaira: "What about my brother? He got to be still out there, lost in the dark, alone!"

Not alone but definitely lost,
Caught within a deadly frost,
Maybe Kaydon's soul will be her cost!
I know for him we shall be weeping,
For who knows what company he is keeping.
Already they have started the reaping.
Slowly into humanity, they are seeping!

Seaira: "I know you may not have much faith, but I believe angels and demons exist just like I believe Kaydon is okay! I don't really blame you. You know so much technical stuff it must be hard for you to believe in something that you cannot gather information from. Having faith in something more allows the soul to accept its fate, all the while knowing they may have no control. Your people are so used to everything being so calculated and everything under control that it's hard to imagine having to accept being a small thread in a big game of tug-of-war. This makes me sad because it must be hard for your souls to accept the light!"

Nurse: "No, child, it is I who is saddened by this! It is this belief that something will always be there to watch over you is why humans are in this mess. Some must simply believe that because something is watching over them that they can just make a mess, and they'll have some kind of holy supervision that will clean up after them. Look at Earth. It is in ruins. It was once one of the most glorious planets ever known! Now it may never return to its former glory all because of humans. Many of my people are starting to think that allowing humans to control the surface of Earth was the worst mistake that we made for the survival of our own. Humans must have known Earth could not remain stable, but instead, they chose to allow this to continue for generations. Many of us believe it is the birth of that mysterious faith that we once thought would save or guide humans from their path of destruction that has led them right into the fire!"

Tears flowed down Seaira's face. "So are you going to kill all of them? What about my brother? What about my friends? Okay, maybe I don't have any friends, but please don't hurt the good ones! I know many have done a lot of bad things, but all of us don't deserve this! Please, I beg you to talk to your people. We can fix things. I'll help in any way I can. You guys can train me to help. I know you can. I'll prove to you at least some are worth saving."

Nurse: "Like I said before, these are trying times! Even if you managed to prove to me that every human was worth saving, I would not be able to stop this train. There is one among us who hates humans more than any, and it is obvious to all what he will do. Sliza is a tyrannical leader. He comes from a long line of war generals. In fact, one of his ancestors was one of the generals who led the fight against your creators. He believes that now you are just like they were, and you will not stop until our planet is consumed. This last war of the surface world, or what humans call World War III, it is really Earth's XI world war, and I fear the XII is coming!"

Sliza a leader of pure hatred.
He will lead the bloodshed.
Seaira's eyes again shut,
Not realizing she's in a rut.
Dreams of her mom and the truck skidding,
Haunting horrors again winning.
Seeing the madness in the dark skies,
At Kaydon, it pries.
When Seaira opens her eyes,
She tears up and cries.

Chapter 4

Herding the Lambs

The alarm bell begun sounding.
Seaira's heart started pounding.
Terror sank in deep,
As their judgment was sleep.
Ironic coming from the sheep,
As if judgment was theirs to reap.

Seaira: "What was that?"

The nurse rushes into the room. "That was the alarm of war. A final decision must have been made!"

That is when Seaira heared the announcement.
War on humans was their punishment,
There was so much resentment,
It seems we may have been too reluctant.
Is anything we do even significant?

A voice over the sound system: "It is time for war! No longer shall we allow the humans we spared to destroy our home. No longer will we allow such reckless beings to control our surface. We gave them peace, and look how they repay us! Now it is the time we retake our home and keep it only ours!"

"That's a quote from Sliza, our great war leader, who will raise us out of the depths of despair we are all in! Soon, our home, Earth, will be all ours again. He signed the document of consecration. All humans must die. May the sun forever warm your scales!"

Seaira: "No . . . please tell me that's not true. Please tell me that was a joke. They are not planning on killing everyone, are they? I'm still here. Are they going to kill me too? That's not fair. I never even had the chance to run, and even if I did, it's not like I would make it far. When they kill me, can you make sure they just get it over with? I don't want to suffer long!"

Nurse: "I'm not going to allow that! As unhappy as I am with humans, I do not wish them all dead, especially you! I can tell your struggle has been greater than most, and yet you beg for the mercy of others. Maybe it's another reckless trait, but it would be an uncommon one. I cannot keep you safe here any longer, and I am afraid I cannot let you leave by the law of the scale. So I must slither you away under the radar. This is not going to be an easy task, but you must trust me and follow my lead to the letter, or we will both end up on the rotting side of life!"

Seaira: "What then? Even if we make it out?"

Nurse: "One step at a time. If we don't make it out, then we don't have to worry about it."

That is when her adventure truly started—the constant looking over the shoulder, the never-ending task of trying to be the salvation of doomed creatures! That is when the tables truly started to turn, and in every seat is one dark choice or another. A game of Russian roulette, but all chambers are loaded. This, though, only feed her ambition for change!

> Concealing Seaira's identity,
> The reptilian hid her indefinitely.
> Using natural camouflage,
> That was the key mirage.

Nurse: "I'll hide you as a prisoner of war! Some know I was talking to you, and after that announcement, they will be expecting me to turn you in now for your death! Knowing how I feel about some humans, some are worried I may do what I am planning. This makes my job harder yet ironically easier. Because they expect me to do what I consider right, they will have me checked on. Once I show them that you're restrained and start walking you down the hall, they will send news that I did not stray. This allows us cover in plain sight because they will then redirect their focus for a short time. You must trust me, child. The things I may say or do once we leave this room may seem cruel, but I have to make the others believe that I hate every human, including you."

Seaira: "Okay, I understand, but I don't know if I'll be able to stop myself from being afraid!"

Nurse: "I know, but lucky for us, your fear will make our illusion more believable. Just remember, I am your friend, and I will protect you! I must now restrain you. Tell me if it's too tight!"

Moving through the halls,
Listening to all the war calls,
Feeling like she's walking into the mouth of jaws
Without any cause.
Led only by faith,
To face the looming wraith.
Closer and closer to the door,
Never again to see a peaceful shore.
That's fate at its core.
The nurse led by plans and science;
Her retribution is her defiance.
The girl is led by the cross
Now into the chaos.

Reptilian guard: "This is not the path to the euthanizing center. Turn around and redirect your path, or I'll call you in as a defector, Salzaria!"

It was within that moment of silence,
Seaira thought it was the end of her alliance.

> Then that strange sound followed
> That made the enemy hollowed
> Then a familiar sound wallowed
> This was the sound of death,
> As the enemy took their last breath!

Seaira, crying and scared: "Salzaria, is that your name?"

Salzaria: "Yes, child, that is my name."

Seaira: "I know I already asked, but what's our plan now?"

Salzaria: "I'll need you to hide."

> Hide in the woods she shall,
> As the lizard goes on the prowl.
> Seaira shall be the lizard's cowl.
> Made it out from the cage of snakes,
> Just to be outside when the ground quakes.
> Seaira out of the dangers beneath,
> Salzaria's weapon close in its sheath.

Salzaria: "I'll go secure a safer location and get you some supplies. I'll have to leave you periodically, but that is only to help. I'll get food and water enough to last you a few days, then I have to see if I can find some good humans who would be suitable to take you in!"

Seaira: "I can stay with you, can't I? We make a good team, and I know you're good!"

Salzaria: "I am not human, child. I cannot meet all you're needs just like a human cannot meet the needs of one of our children."

Seaira: "But I don't want you to leave me. What if someone comes to hurt me, or what if I can't do this on my own?"

Salzaria: "I know this is scary, but you have to be strong now. Not all humans will help you. Some would sooner let you die. I must find the right humans. And having you with me only creates greater risk. You need to trust me once again. I only mean to help you."

Seaira: "I've known you were good before I even met you! I know you only mean to help."

Salzaria: "How could you have known I was good before you even met me? I could have been anybody. I could have wanted you dead!"

Seaira, smiling: "I told you I can sense light and darkness. You may be a little lost, but your soul is bright. So you are good!"

Chapter 5

Snakebite

Fiery meteors fall from the sky.
So full of rage, I wonder why.
Darkness rises as the ground quakes.
These terrors haunt her before she wakes.
Caught within the shroud of dark,
Horrors forever leaving their mark.

Salzaria: "I have found them, the ones in which I have been looking! You must trust them as you would trust me."

Seaira: "But where are you going to go? You cannot return home."

Salzaria: "I will still be with you! Now follow me and stay close."

In the woods again, they shall be,
The lizard and the girl who cannot see.
Seaira was alone outside the camp,
Fear in her gut like a cramp.
The scale parted from the little human,
So Seaira called for help and raised a beacon.
The man cries
As he looked into her eyes,

For she is more than a surprise!

Man: "Hey, there's a little girl over here. Clear the area and send for the doctor. She may need aid!"

Seaira: "It's okay. I'm not hurt. I just need somewhere to stay. I won't be any trouble, I promise!"

Man: "I know you won't. We have a few other kids back at camp, so you can have some fun with them! Looks like it's been a while since you had fun. Oh, my name is Brian. Once the doctor gets here, she'll check you out, and then we will show you to your room!"

> Seaira may have met many humans.
> Moments of peace can cast many illusions.
> But the small group Salzaria has chosen
> Has a fate already woven!
> This maybe the start of Seaira's fight.
> Here, she does not find answers for the blight,
> But she does regain her might
> While training with her sight.

Seaira: "I get my own room?"

Brian: "Yes, you get your own room. We got plenty of room for you! The doctor, Kim, is just right there. Do you see her?"

Seaira: "I can't see. I'm blind and albino. I was born this way."

Brian: "Oh my! I'll just lead you to her! Don't worry. Everything is going to be okay!"

Dr. Kim: "Hi, I'm Kim. I'll be tending to your medical needs. Are you hurt in anyway? And are there any allergies or sensitivities that I should be made aware of?"

Seaira: "Hi, I'm Seaira! I only have a couple of scratches. I'm kind of clumsy. I'm also blind, and I'm albino. And I just lost everybody. I don't know where everyone is. I'm hoping to find my brother, Kaydon! Oh, as for allergies, I'm allergic to mayo."

Dr. Kim, with a smile: "Hopefully, your brother, Kaydon, is already here. If not, we can help! And are you allergic, or you just don't like mayo?"

Seaira: "Well, I don't like mayo. Therefore, my body doesn't like mayo, so I'm allergic!"

Dr. Kim: "That's not how allergies work, but I'll patch you up! We will show you to your room now. You must be tired. There're good people here. We will take care of you."

> Seaira was seen wandering the grass
> As the days come and pass.
> But it was the nights that brought horror,
> As she would dream of more terror.
> Once again found screeching
> While Seaira is sleeping.
> Curiosity brought them creeping,
> now they found what they have been seeking.
> Maybe this was just fate,
> But they took the bait.
> As Seaira sleeps, they wait!
> It is time to tell the tale
> Of her friend with the scale,
> For without her, the enemy will prevail!

Seaira: "Salzaria, I see your people and my people fighting, but this time, something worse than war may be coming true, something bigger than I think any of us are ready for!"

Dr. Kim: "Who is Salzaria? And who are the other people?"

With no time for preparation,
She must warn them of the coming devastation.
This was Seaira's revelation!

Seaira: "Wait, where am I again?"

Dr. Kim: "You're in your room, remember?"

Seaira: "Oh yeah, my room, and you're that nice human doctor!"

Dr. Kim: "Human? I think you're going to have to answer more questions!"

Seaira: "It's okay. I'm supposed to talk anyways. You see, I didn't exactly stumble on your camp by accident. I had help, and my friend who helped me isn't human. Her skin is rougher and has ridges with little sharp spots she calls scales. Apparently, they shed them from time to time. Isn't that cool! But sadly, their people are mad at us, not Salzaria but her other people. Salzaria would like to speak to all of you and help us in any way she can. I guess I am her reference, as you adults call it."

As Seaira finally broke a smile,
She left the doctor in denial!
Then they set up a meeting,
Thinking it was an imaginary friend they are greeting.
Well, it was to their surprise
When her reptilian friend did arise!
If it were not for Seaira's voice,
Her friend would have had little choice!

Salzaria: "We must speak! I know it is all hard to take in right now, but we must move through the steps of acceptance quickly, for there are very urgent matters we must attend! For I fear we are facing a threat that neither reptilian nor human can survive! Sadly, the threat is the hasty, naive action of ourselves!"

Brian: "You can't be real. Am I asleep? Please, someone pinch me! What should I do? Should I shoot it?"

Salzaria: "I am no threat. I assure you!"

Dr. Kim: "That is yet to be seen!"

Seaira: "If it was not for my friend, I would not be alive! I was in their base, and they were going to kill me, then she killed them! She found you for me knowing she could not help me alone. Please listen to her. I know you must be scared, but please listen. She is a friend, I promise. Please, you must listen!"

Brian: "How can we trust them if they had been in hiding this whole time? What if they are using your trusting heart to lure all of us to our death? You have a kind heart, and you believe. This I do not doubt. It is the intention of this lizard raptor that I cannot trust!"

Seaira: "I promise one thing. If we don't start getting along, what is coming for all of us will not care if we are ready! They will not wait for us to be friends and team up, if it even matters anymore! I know you don't believe me. You all think I am some sort of crazy. All I can do is try, you know. Where I stand now, it seems there is no hope. Even if you all start hugging and pouring up tea, we probably do not have time to drink it. We are all going to die!"

Chapter 6

Dark Descent

Even with all Seaira's new friends, she seeks one other.
This one just happens to be her brother!
But this mark she cannot find,
For the darkness has Kaydon in a bind!
Three weeks prior, he started his dark descent!
For his story, I am sad to present.
He blames Seaira for his pain!
That is why her efforts will go in vain!
He is already too far to be swayed.
I fear he will belong to the fade!
He left her in that cave.
She, he cared not to save!

Kaydon: "Hello, Seaira, is that you?"

Distant, unclear voice: "Yes, it's me. I am over here!"

Kaydon: "I told you to stay in that cave! It's too dangerous out here! Why didn't you listen to me, and how did you manage to follow me? Wait . . . you're not . . . !"

A demonic voice: "No, I am not, but how lucky I am to find such a prize! *Oh* . . . how I can smell that wretched girl through thee! Thou, too, must be close. Come on, tell me. Where is she?"

> The hysterical laughter
> Has made Kaydon realize his disaster!
> He told so many things,
> Wondering what this dark knight brings!
> Torture is part of its dark prize,
> So Kaydon didn't tell any lies!
> Demons love teary eyes.

Kaydon: "What are you?"

A demonic voice: "No worries. I am a good guy! I'm an angel!"

Kaydon: "You can't be an angel. You wouldn't take the form of my . . ."

Demon, resuming its chaotic laughter: "I guess I am not fully lying since that beautiful moment when I led one-third of us into the Darkness!

Demon:

> "Since then, thou humans
> Call us demons!
> Thou consider us evil.
> Thou think us so deceitful.
> What stupid people!
> Now I will be honest to thee, pest.
> I am ready to settle in and nest!
> But just before I lay thee down to rest,
> Information I need and the best!
> Why do thee look so sad?
> Oh, how thou have been so bad.
> Greetings, I am the master of the mad.
> Come relax with me and Vlad!"

Kaydon: "Just stop! I'll tell you anything!"

Master of Madness: "Where is thy sister?"

Kaydon: "I ditched her in a cave! Why? What would you want with her?"

Master of Madness:

"Oh, you see, she can sense us in the dark.
That's why Death has made his mark!
Thou may think I am upset,
But running into thee I do not regret.
Now tell me something, my little dear.
What do humans truly fear?"

Kaydon: "Dragons! People fear dragons!"

Brought up a nonexistent creature,
He thought would brighten his future.
Demons may be demented,
But many raw ideas they have invented!

Kaydon: "They're massive creatures like dinosaurs with wings, scaly skin, big heads, teeth, and claws! They can also breathe fire!"

Master of Madness: "Maybe this I can do. But breathing fire? That is boring! Angels like fire, and it's so predictable! Instead, you can spew darkness! The cold darkness devours like fire, but it's much more interesting to watch!"

The demonic master can be seen orchestrating his madness with a bounce to his step, a smile on his face, and joy deep within his soul!

Master of Madness: "So I need lots of bones, flesh, and scales! First, some bone-rendering flesh, then it is time. Flesh is rendered from bone and, finally, the scales.

Master of Madness:

> "Can thee hear them rising?
> How they think, they are the ones doing the surprising.
> It's time their army gets a resizing.
> I'll creep up ever so slowly.
> They are the same as thee mostly,
> Just so unaware.
> All those scales just right there,
> This is hardly even fair.
> Their war, they never even got to declare.
> Me and thou, though, boy, make a great pair.
> Oh, how I am glad I have thee in my snare!"

Sliza: "Span out, find any and all humans, and end them where they stand. Remember, this is not a rehabilitation. This is an annihilation!"

Master of Madness: "Thou got that right, my scaly friend.

> How I wonder how many ways thee bend,
> I guess thou have never seen this as thy end.
> But thou may continue to pretend,
> That thy soul is only on a lend.
> It, back to the Light, we shall send
> When there is nothing left to mend.
> Hey, look, they just shot me.
> Now that is truly blasphemy.
> How funny, now they running.
> I guess they're not a fan of my punning.
> It's okay. I'll round them up and continue humming,
> Flush out the trash with some plumbing.
> Now that I got the scales, boy,
> It's time to turn thee into my new favorite toy.
> Do not worry. I still love thee, Ceverus.
> Please don't look so serious."

Ceverus, the three-headed hound,
Since he met Madness, a friend he has found.
Together they would eat
The corpses at their feet.
Kaydon could never get away.
For him, we shall pray.

"Time to give this boy exactly what he deserves.
Hold still. I need to rip out thy spine to stretch the nerves!"

Too young years of age
To be on this cursed page.
Snapping Kaydon off at the knees
To make sure he never flees.
Tearing limb from limb,
This fate is truly grim.
Screams travel a distance
But doesn't matter of their existence,
For this creature cares not for repentance.
Breaking every bone
To alter its shape and tone.
Gathering meat for the muscle
To its movement was no hustle.
Then the scales for the skin
Ripped from the dead reptilian,
Corpses that lay there by the million.
Then was the breaking of the jaw.
This, I am glad, Seaira never saw.
Adding teeth, horns, and claws,
This is pain without pause.
Never to know a peaceful harmony,
For he is now known as the Dragon of Agony.
Pieced together with dark synergy,
This is truly a demonic symphony.
Traced through his chip technology,
Through its waves and its energy.

When the chip humans did place,
No one expected evil's trace.
Another accidental human disgrace,
The dragon weighing multiple tons.
Regeneration costs daughters and sons.
People fire bullets from their gun
Until emptied, then they run.
Again and again, Kaydon does feast,
Slowly turning into the beast.
His mind is gone, to say the least!

Chapter 7

The Light

In a once great city, a battle has begun.
What war has anyone truly won?
Even if they all finally work together,
I fear their fates are sealed forever!
For every time the gates are open,
An intelligent species rests, their fate woven!
Seaira and her group of reliable friends
Finally found a way to make amends.
Now together to reap what fate rends,
May they all meet again when fate ends!
Reptilian's early intention
Has prolonged this divine intervention.
Now there is no stopping this annihilation.
Earth needs to be rid of its desecration.
Now starts the consecration!
Now starts the purification!
That night, the ground shook.
No one dared to go and look.
Then came the knock.
There, they stood on the other side of the lock.

Seaira felt them as they raised.
If they got her, they would be praised.

Seaira: "Don't answer that!"

Dr. Kim: "Look, it's just some kids. I am opening the door!"

Seaira: "They're not just kids!"

Dr. Kim: "I can see them. They're harmless, I promise!"

As she opened the door,
She realized that they were more.
It was their smile;
They were vile,
Maybe even senile!
It is when they were let in
That the terror starts to begin.
Then they showed their true form,
Then outside stood a swarm.
Seaira's friends have been infiltrated.
She stood there devastated.
They ripped the human doctor apart,
For her friends were not supernaturally smart.
It was in that hysteria
That she ran with Salzaria.
Brian, being one of the last,
Looked at Seaira for her to go past.

Brian: "No more children will die on my watch! I thought it was all over.
I thought I knew evil! Maybe I could not save my own. Maybe I could not
save the others. But I will save you!"

Once again, Seaira fleeing from a bloody scene, feeling a dark shadow
approach! Seaira was cornered, scared, pushed back, and beaten! Then
she heards the beast's roar on the horizon!

Salzaria: "Stay strong. Move fast! There is much going on here. We have to go now!"

Seaira: "You don't even know, do you? You still don't believe? After all we been through! We can't run from this storm. I have to go to him. It's the only way!"

> With no time for chatter,
> Structures around them shatter.
> Rocks keep crashing
> From the demons thrashing.
> Seaira's friend did push,
> Afraid Seaira would go mush.
> The rock destined to fall
> Was not meant for Seaira at all.
> But Salzaria, her friend, it did maul.
> Then closer came the roar
> From the dragon as it would soar.
> Into a wagon she went,
> A metal wagon that is bent.
> As she continued to weep,
> The beast continued to creep.
> Speaking into her mind,
> Hoping for answers to find.

Seaira: "I can't let this continue. I lost too much. I got to tell him I still care. I got to tell him that it doesn't matter that he abandoned me once, that I love him for standing up for me all those times that he did! I can't let him keep hurting. I can't let him continue in this pain. But his soul . . . it's so dark!"

> Leapt from the wagon
> To confront her brother, the dragon.
> It was Seaira's love for her assassin that made him most deadly.
> Seaira acted so friendly.
> Lucky his teeth were so thick,
> Because he blew her wick out quick!

Seaira: "I see it, the Light! It calls for me. The warmth, it wants me to ascend!"

Seaira: "Now I remember what I wanted to ask! Because in that moment, I looked down out of curiosity, then as I hurried toward the Light, I felt an overwhelming sadness! All the souls down there, they all can't be evil! Why didn't they ascend?"

Fate:

> "For now, Death has not yet risen.
> Words have not yet been written.
> We will just keep reading.
> I am not trying to be deceiving.
> All will be made clear.
> Thy answers are near!"

Chapter 8

Unstable Equilibrium

We've been battling to maintain an equilibrium,
For all life lives in an unstable aquarium.
How do we beat such a feat?
How do we ensure our enemies' defeat?
Thus, it's why we must meet!
You see, I, too, have questions.
Maybe we can teach each other lessons!

Seaira, in her mind: *"Wow . . . I can see so much now. I must be in space!
There are all the things I once dreamed of seeing, all just right there!"*

Seaira: Oh, I guess this is when I was first able to see. Too bad, so much
was destroyed! I seen so much fire. Even fiery rocks were falling onto Earth
as I was leaving! I guessed those were meteors!

Fate:

Those were not meteors at all.
Those were not meteors that thee saw fall.

Seaira: "Salzaria, is that you?"

Seaira: *Oh, this must be where I saw Salzaria on the stairs!*

Salzaria: "Yes, child, I did as you instructed. I moved toward the Light! For a while now, I've been struggling on these stairs!"

Seaira: "Interesting. I go up them easily! It's okay, though, if you're struggling. I'm going to wait for you! Well, it would only be fair. You waited for me many times!"

Salzaria: "I can see the top, but yet no famed gate."

Seaira: "They're here. They are all here!"

Salzaria: "What do you mean?"

Seaira: "Beneath the stairs, I can feel . . . everyone! We are here!"

Salzaria, as she stood in awe: "There it is! Do we just walk through?"

Seaira: "No, we jump!"

Seaira: "Why is my story written so strange?"

Fate:

> That is one of the things we must question more.
> That is one question I've had before.
> Nonetheless,
> I will confess.
> We shall continue reading then address
> All our questions,
> All our confessions!

Seaira: "Well, that certainly answers a lot wait . . . Are you writing all this down? You don't seem to be writing exactly what you say, but when I look, the words turn to exactly what I understand them to be. How is that?"

Fate: "I write everything down as it happens! The ink I use is different than any other. I write like how an angel speaks . . . in tongues! I write in my understanding of language, and when thou read it, the ink turns to thy understanding, in this case, being the human language known as English!"

Seaira: "Oh, that is so cool! Can I try?"

Fate: "Thou must never touch the quill! It was made for me many years ago, and my power has been surging through it ever since. Thou most likely would not survive its touch! It is now only meant to be wielded by its owner. Like the fiery blade of the Angel of Wrath or Death's scythe, they have used their chosen instruments for so long it would either burn or consume any who dares to wield what is not theirs. Never mind that for now though. We must keep reading. If we read to where we are, we will see our conversation as it is being said. Then we may find the answers we seek!"

Seaira: "Okay, I understand now."

> We go on with her own story.
> I do not know how to tell her I am sorry.
> But our unusual meeting
> Is not without reasoning.
> For once I'm lost for words,
> Usually they come to me in herds.
> Yet she is not ready.
> She is not even steady.
> Leaping through the gates of fire
> To see the haven of hope's desire.
> Surprised, Seaira was to find
> An empty city not how it was designed.
> The guards stand and weep,
> Wallowing in misery of failure to keep.
> In their hearts, it did seep.
> Long ago, it did reap.
> Walking through the city so hollow,
> That is when I told her to follow.

Disappointment is met with happiness.
For now, she is absent of loneliness.
For those who have rotted on her trail
Stand before her and hail.
For now, why I tell her this tale,
Those of whom she asked,
Asked to be saved, but who shall be tasked?
For this girl, I must meet.
Summon her here, I must and greet.
Her gift of sight
Gives her an unusual might.
It was shortly after the family greeting
That I summoned her to this meeting.
I told her to read what was written,
To read to where she was bitten.
Now that our reading
Has almost caught up to my writing,
It's time to tell her why we are fighting.

Chapter 9

Angelic Debate

Just before Seaira's arrival,
A decision was made by a Light disciple.
Judgment falls from the angels;
Fire rains from all angles.
I do not yet know if the dots are connected,
For I do not know what is truly affected.
I'll tell you the recent events.
I'll tell you who repents.
I cannot see the why or how,
But I can read to the now.
Maybe we can peek,
Then we may find what we seek.
These are the events that have transpired
Just before Seaira's body expired.
The meteors she saw falling toward Earth
Are not natural at birth.
First, she must know the events leading.
These actions then are the seeding.
My heart is ripped and is now bleeding!

Fate: "Just before thou arrived, the angels made their decision. Those meteors were not meteors at all! This happens at the beginning of every judgment. Angels fall as demons rise. Then Life and Death awaken! But Life has not woken in one hundred and eleven judgments. Sadly, Life is weak from the pain of all his children! He feels every emotion. With every cut, he is paralyzed with their pain. He even feels agony from deep within the Darkness!"

Crazed angel spitting madness: "How could we believe the humans would be any different? The only reason some remain faithful is because their history is littered with higher intervention! They would be like all the others who have fallen before them—faithless and full of sin! Even now, crippled and struggling, facing a force they cannot defeat, they still choose to sin against their own. They still kill one another! It was inevitable one day that those born with scales would turn their back on the humans they swore to protect!"

Broken angel within its sadness: "It seems to me, brother, that thou have lost faith. Do thee not believe anymore? Do thee really want the gates to be open? Have thee lost so much hope that it is time for judgment? Can we not spare them once more and hope this chaos comes to its end? Death has been regenerating with every cleansing. Every time we lose just as many as we gain, and the darkness forever thickens! This judgment may be our last. This may be the move that ends us! How can we make this decision so lightly? We must consult the scribe. We must speak with Life!"

Crazed angel: "How can thee be so naive? There is no hope for any of them, just like those before. We must not wait any longer, for the ones who can be saved may also be forever lost in the Darkness!"

Angel of Wrath:

> "Then we shall open the gate,
> Hope a miracle is in our fate.
> Now we shall rain down.
> Father, please do not frown.
> We fight for thee, the bright crown."

Seaira: Fate, are you an angel?

Fate: I am no angel, nor am I a normal son or daughter! I am a fragment of Life! Life always feels, hears, sees, and knows seemingly everything! Over time, this burden became heavy, and he shared some of his sight and knowledge they were much of a distraction. He still feels, hears, and sees, but I am a fraction of his knowledge! I can also listen to the calls of his children and see through their eyes as he can! Since these pieces were placed into my vessel or since my creation, I've had an impulse to write all that I know. To write this knowledge, I was gifted a quill. Then was born the belief of purpose, noticing events that would have been worse if not for previous coincidental events, making magical moments possible! These magical moments humans call miracles! The events that happen just before are believed to be fateful. Since I am the one who writes these fateful events, Life saw it fitting to name me Fate!

> I am like the words in a book,
> Only to be seen when you take a closer look.
> Seaira has seen two apocalypses on her way.
> Now the last one is the first double judgment day!

Seaira: You believe yourself to be some kind of tool, don't you? Well, let me tell you, mister. I can tell you are much more than that! You already have grown on me because I've personally witnessed your character for who you are! You care about everything just as he does, and you write to give knowledge!"

Fate: Thy heart is strong, but I am merely knowledge with arms to write.

Seaira: As a friend, if I hear that once more, I will kick you!

Fate: "Now just listen. We are close to the now! Then we may understand!"

> You see, this has happened before.
> Every being thought they were more.
> Judgment rains from the angels;
> Fire falls from all angles.

You see, there was no stopping what's next.
Now their fate is sealed and forever hexed.

The fate of humans was unseen, as was the fate of many before thee and as our fate is thereafter. Shall thee rise into the purifying light to face burning judgment, or shall thee descend into the bitter, cold Darkness? Will thee quiver once awakened from blissful ignorance, or will thee stand while shrouded in agony?

Chapter 10

Judgment

This is a war forever raging
Ever since the very beginning.
Life and Death fight for their cause,
Both without a moment to pause.
Many fall to their sin.
They fall with their kin.
I fear we are too late.
They have sealed their fate.
The angels have spoken.
Judgment, the angels have chosen.
Both gates are now open.
This is what's forever woven.
Death has again awoken.

An angel's wrath is vicious, relentless, and unforgiving. They melt down resources needed to construct basic weapons and armor. Melting a firing squad led just to make needlelike projectiles, followed by a wave of holy fire burning and purifying the guilty in its wake. That end, though, is a better end than those tormented by the horsemen who rise out of the Darkness. They and their armies freeze body, mind, and soul only to tear pieces away slowly, allowing you to regenerate. In Death's perspective, why would he throw away perfect rechargeable batteries? In the end, humans and reptilians alike will only be fragments of what they were.

Seaira: Hey, the page, it's blank now. Does that mean my story is over?

Fate: Oddly, I do not know. Everything seems to be still . . . for a moment!

Ding . . . Ding . . . Ding . . . Ding . . . Ding . . . Ding . . . Ding . . .

Fate: The great bell of Life . . . our father is calling. We all must answer! The angels must return home. Life has to speak with all his children! I will go see his instruction. I will return soon when I know more. I will call the angels, but I know they cannot hear me over all the screams.

I, Fate, leave the room and proceed to the throne to receive word!

Seaira: I must get them. I must tell the angels their father is calling. They can't hear him. I must go, and I must go now.

Salzaria: I will go with you. You're not alone in this. I will gladly again stand by your side.

Seaira: Thank you! You never would have guessed the day we met that one day we would be on a mission to find angels!

Salzaria: The day we met changed me because you have changed me, and for that, I thank you!

> Seaira, with her message, did descend
> To save a dark world with her friend,
> Hoping there is something left to mend.
> Following the sound of screams,
> Following the sound of broken dreams,
> For that's where the angels are falling.
> The screams block their father's calling,
> Who can hear with so many children bawling,
> When so many young souls are sobbing.

Upon arriving at Earth, her home,
On the search for angels, she must not roam.
She arrives where needs are dire,
To be loved, a child's one desire.
This, some never knew prior
To the angels with their fire.
Out of the Darkness, demons run amok.
In their twisted minds, they are stuck.
Seaira's first stop, what luck!
Out of the black, evil rises.
They are always full of surprises.
Out of the Darkness, when they shall rise,
What they do next, you can summarize.
They destroy all of creation,
Causing deep laceration.
They think it a wonderful sensation
When blood sprays from the evisceration.
They come at the world's devastation,
Starting with a game of domination,
Before Death orders the obliteration.

Master of Madness:
I am the Master of Madness.
I am the one that brings all thy sadness.
We are the definition of insanity,
Coming to torment all of humanity.
Here to redefine agony,
We are those who rise out of the dark.
We are those with the hunting aspect of a shark.
We are the monsters from the deep,
Collecting all thy souls to keep.
When we finally lay thee down to sleep,
The ground shall quake as we rise from the Darkness.
Compared to Death and his snake, all are powerless.

Thou shall quiver at our sight.
Thou shall shiver to our cold bite.
As we give thee a last kiss good night,
Thou may think me crazy.
Yes, just a little maybe.
But thou all are just so easy,
Pleading, "Please don't kill me."
We will freeze thee in thy tracks.
This is just the first wave of attacks!
Thy ignorance is our bliss.
We will make holes in thee like Swiss.
Before we give the last kiss,
We will rip flesh like bacon.
Thou are truly forsaken!

Fiery meteors fall from the sky,
So full of rage, I wonder why.
Landing with fury, turning things to dust.
Rising out of the flames, the angels we trust.
Revenge for the innocent is their lust.
Purifying evil, it is just.
First to rise burns bright,
For he is the wrath of the light.
They have had enough of this desecration.
Now they lay down the final consecration.
Now there is no reconciliation
For all walk into their own annihilation.

Angel of Wrath:
I am the Angel of Wrath.
I shall burn all guilty in my path.
I am the embodiment of rage.
I'm the one who puts the madness back in its cage.
For too long have we heard innocent screams,
Too long have we been cracking at the seams!

We will get justice for the pain of the innocent.
For now, it is time to rain down our judgment.
Holy fire is thy punishment.
We are the light in this dark shroud.
Our task is burning the crowd.
For we are the burning legions,
Coming to burn all thy heathens.
Thou may not think we have our reasons,
But look at all these treasons.
Few will be able to stand the coming flames,
For all their sins, for all their shames.
Darkness rises as humanities curse.
As the light prepares Earth's hearse,
Death forever filling his soul purse!

Angels and demons now clashing—
Angels with their fiery bashing,
Demons using their twisted thrashing.
One angel gets cornered into a rock,
Melts his staff into one block.
Staff and rock is now hammer;
Onto a demonic skull is its first slammer.

Seaira struggles to tell the angels of their father's calling. They fall, collect
the innocent, and rise just to fall again and again, collecting more to bring
to the Light's safe haven. Seaira can see the children latching on to the
limbs of the angels just before they ascend! Seaira screeches out and is
not heard or seen. She hides only to rise when the time is right, to make
another attempt at her mission.

Again and again, her message is not received.
They feel as if they were being deceived,
Now only if they believed.
Sadly, the angels all lost faith and broke
Their faith in love up in smoke.

A message, Life has spoken.
Now I know because he has awoken.
Hopefully, Seaira does not break
Hope for all our sake,
Because Life is now awake,
And his words we need to take!

Chapter 11

Era of Pain

When anxieties begin to wane,
That's when they rise to rain,
Thus beginning the era of pain.
Thou may die but never rot,
For thy soul is forever caught.
Put back together by thy reaper,
Flesh and bone are thy sleeper.
Seaira is a lucky one,
For she died before this began.
But now from the Light, she has fled,
Back to Earth amid the bloodshed.
Somehow, I know she is a link.
Pray for that in the Darkness, she does not sink.
For the pitch-black souls are countless,
But those left fighting for the Light are lifeless.
As Seaira hides in the shadows,
She hears whispers in the dark meadows!

Crazed demon:

> I love catching those who are sneaking.
> What is it that thee be seeking?
> Is it thee trying to find a place to be sleeping?
> Before thou can go for a nap,
> I got to milk some sap!
> We make sweet honey
> In ways we find funny.
> Soon it will never again be sunny.
> But after the reaper makes its mends,
> Don't worry, we can still be friends.
> We can be together forever till fate ends,
> When we all see what fate rends!

> Angels burn everything in their wake.
> Demons leave pools of pain like a lake.
> Angels hear the message, for it is not fake.
> Demons screech as they burn.
> Angels squirm as they turn.
> Darkness disintegrates to ash,
> As the light falls to Death's lash.

Angel of Wrath:

Forward! All evil burns now before Death arrives with his horsemen. We cannot fight him. And all these demons, show them our wrath, show them justice for their treacherous ways. Now it's time for them to scream!

> Arriving on Earth is Death,
> Here to collect every breath.
> He and his horsemen now alive,
> Here to slaughter and thrive.
> A soul collection he does drive,
> Consuming all flesh, bone, and energy in his wake.
> Seaira, stay out of his way, for goodness' sake.

I wish she did not return.
For her, I have great concern.
Yet another red riverbed,
Though expected with all the bloodshed.
Once again, the Darkness is well-fed.
Screams from every edge of Earth's crust,
To serve Death and demon bloodlust.
Tearing hope from our chest
Just to wear it on their dark crest.

Death: Now it is time for madness. Rise from thy ashes, my armies. It's time to devour all. We will consume everything in our wake. Nothing will be able to stand against me, for I am Death. I am the end!

Death's long reach stretches across the globe.
Death, with his blade, wearing that damned black robe.
As Death rises, with him rise the horsemen made from Death's dark soul,
To be his eyes in every corner to direct his army's goal.

Built from Death's rage is the horseman of War, crazed and forever thirsty for battle, led completely on the impulse of bloodshed. Some may say for these horsemen, battle is as easy as breathing, but the horsemen do not breathe!

Next, the horseman known as Pestilence, born from all the impure imperfections Death disposed of and then combined all into this one vile being! This one prefers its prey squirming as they spew their own insides out!

Last was the horseman Famine, born from Death's own need to feed, to consume everything! Even his own is not safe, for this one eats for his armies and is the dark's main source of nutrients!

Each takes a corner of Earth with a total of ten thousand, thousand horsemen terrorizing everything in their path. Dying is no longer an option, for all that is needed is the strains of blood left from one's body to reconstruct them from raw materials.

Evil blinded in the light,
Bright flames hold off the blight.
How long can they hold?
Fire dies out quick in breathless cold.
The darkness, a deceitful mold.
Angel's molten core turns to a rocky crust
Just before they're shattered into dust.
Only a few left; hold they must.
The clash of claw iron and steel,
As time continues to turn on its wheel.
Scared of the future I am to seek,
Scared to just look and have a peek.
Does this mean I have grown weak?
They must hear the wish of Life.
Before Death is done playing with his scythe,
They must hear our father's decision.
The light must make a dark incision,
The first task in a long time with a just mission.

Chapter 12

Wish of Life

The last few shout
As the lights went out.
All the stars are dead,
Their fate long ago read.
Their light's final reach
Has made its last breech.
Few had the sight
Of the stars' last light.
The sky has now darkened.
Angels now know they have been beckoned.
They must return home;
No longer can they roam.
A message to me, Life has spoken.
They he must see now that he has awoken.
The message they must receive.
It is in Seaira, they must believe.
The end may be near.
This is what I fear!
I know there will be a quest.
We must give it our best.
I wish this was just a test.

Now I know why her story hasn't ended.
I know why it continued after she ascended.
She may be the one picked
To enter the dark crypt.

Seaira:

Stop! You must stop fighting.
You must see in a different lighting.
You must hear the prayer Life is reciting.
He prays for his children to return.
Too many children he has placed in an urn.
He has awoken with great concern.
You all must return home and learn.
How do you think I know of Fate?
Do I really look like some kind of bait?
Before you continue, just wait.
You may not listen to what I have to say,
But Life, our father, will show you the way.
Please listen to him if you may!

Angel of Wrath:

How does she know of Fate and our father?
Her words, I did not heed or bother.
She must have descended from above.
She descended as a dove.
We must alter our tone
And return to the throne.
Remember not to scorn.
We are lucky she was born!

Now gathering in the great hall,
They all gather—come one, come all.
How I wish we were joining for a ball.

We all gather to hear Life's wish,
Hoping it's not another bitter served dish.
Holding our breath for when Life speaks,
Holding for answers that all seeks.

Life: As thou may know for many years, I have not left the throne. The pain of all my children has pinned me to this location. I have watched as everything we have ever hoped for slips away. I've seen even the strongest break and lose hope. It hurts me so to see so much pain and not be able to embrace my children!

Waves of pain over and over
How can we ever recover

Life: I am unable to battle in my current condition.
This is why I have created a mission!
For to reach our united vision,
The light must make a dark incision.
Before the final clash or collision,
Who will lead our bright legion?
Who will drive our siege engine?
Who will lead with the best intention?
Who can bring the darkness to a bright intervention?
Who can gather my lost children
For their first ascension?

Again father has paused
We can all see what this pain caused

Life's prayer: Please stop their pain . . . Please bring them home!

A little voice speaks, . . .Oh how she has grown.
All the other voices silence is shown.
What happened next caught me by surprise,
As she raises up like the sunrise.

Seaira:

> I will take up the repenting scrolls.
> I will collect the repenting souls.
> No longer will they suffer.
> I'll bring them home to you, our father.
> I am sorry to you, my mother,
> But I must do what's right
> And lead the armies of the Light.
> I can sense the evil in the dark,
> So I can be the bright flame's spark!
>
> Legion after legion, they all stand,
> The bright legions is their brand .
> Humans, reptilians, and others alike
> Join the angels for when they strike.
> All the heroes over the ages,
> All the heroes from different pages
> Soon swear loyalty.
> Heart is the true power of divinity.
> Out of one gate and into another,
> Everyone backing up each other.
> With Seaira at the lead,
> This is the one win we need!

Chapter 13

Into the Darkness

The Light's soul huntress
Now enters the Darkness.
Angels moving in a flash,
With their shield bash.
Fury and relentlessness,
No sign of cowardness.
Many demons are burning
By thy legion that are surging.
In the dark, the light shines bright.
Many demons see their sight
And soon join the fight.
They must hold for what's right.
Seaira breaks away and journeys deeper,
Right past the dark deceiver.
She finds many on her list,
But they no longer really exist.
Piece by piece, they were broken.
Each piece, another demon's token.

Seaira falls off her feet.
Some of them take a seat.
She knows this is a leap.
Feeling defeated, she begins to weep.
Then a chill goes up her spine,
As she senses one from her vine.
Seaira looks back.
The light dims in the black.
Many have become a demon's snack.
When she turns around,
She has been found.
Her brother, the beast,
She already was once a dragon's feast.
He looks her in the eye.
The long pause, then her cry,
Hoping the end isn't nigh.
Checking the list for his naming,
He is there on the list of the repenting,
Her heart already accepting.

Dragon of Agony:

May I ask forgiveness of you, my sister?
I used to blame you for my anger.
Too long have I been here,
I hope you can see I am sincere.

Seaira, with a smile: I forgave you long ago. You saved me so many times,
but you only killed me once!

As she hugs the dragon's skull,
He tells her to hop on and to not fall.
Many more in the dark to seek,
Time is on one fast leak.
With her brother, she did fly,
Soaring through the dark sky.

Many souls are hard to find,
But from battle, they stayed behind.
Gathering them becomes easy under her accord.
Now the challenge is getting past the horde.
Heading toward the light so dim,
Again, their fate is looking grim.
She fears they will be rip off every limb. Evil eyes glow in the dark.
Death, at the flank, has found his mark.
Angels try and make a path,
But many have fallen in this bloodbath.
Seaira's brother sets her on the ground,
For his fate, he has found.
Fighting to reach the angels,
Fighting through all that mangles.
Again, reaching the gate,
A miracle weaved in fate.
She looks and sees many survivors.
The face she doesn't see is her brother's.
Just out of the gate, Death stands,
With her brother in his hands.
Death points his blade at her brother's chin,
For he is the reason she did win.
He speaks but one word.
This, she wishes she never heard.

Death: Treachery!

Death's blade is like a fang of a black widow. It destroys its prey before
Death consumes it!

As her brother begins to rot,
She stands there without a thought,
Her heart is torn to pieces
As her brother's life ceases.

Seaira: Kaaaydon . . . !

Life and I can no longer wait.
We rush toward the gate.
I notice he moves with less weight.
Seaira rushes with the repenting ones
As Life greets them with seven suns.

We hear less screams.
Their pain no longer haunts his dreams.
He is no longer cracking at the seams.
Leading his children into the Light,
I saw his thoughts shine bright.
All his children, we did save.
I know he is about to do something brave,
Because he looked at me, Fate,
And ordered me to close the gate.
Follow his orders, I must,
For in our father, I trust.
Then he seals the gate so it will not bust.
Standing outside the gates alone,
Neither king on their throne!

Death: You are Life. You are the beginning! I am Death. I am the end!

CPSIA information can be obtained
at www.ICGtesting.com
Printed in the USA
JSHW020713270623
43834JS00003B/15

9 781664 194571